To all of the people who inspire me.
(You know who you are.)

Library of Congress Cataloging-in-Publication Data on file.
ISBN 978-0-578-49462-3

Printed in China

Let's Make a Cake!

by **Heidi Schrack**

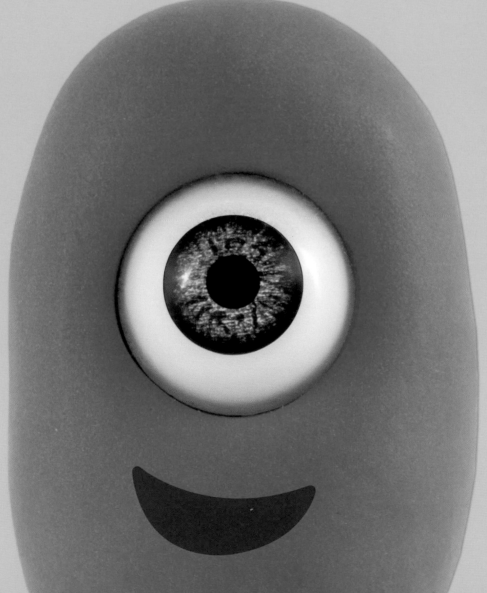

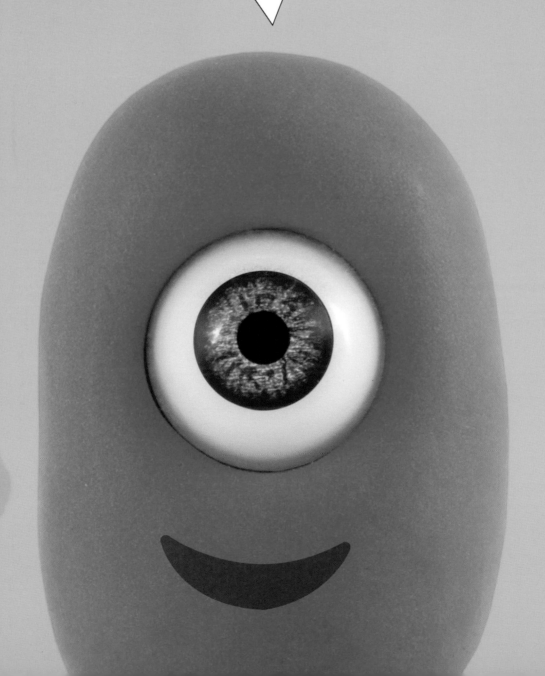

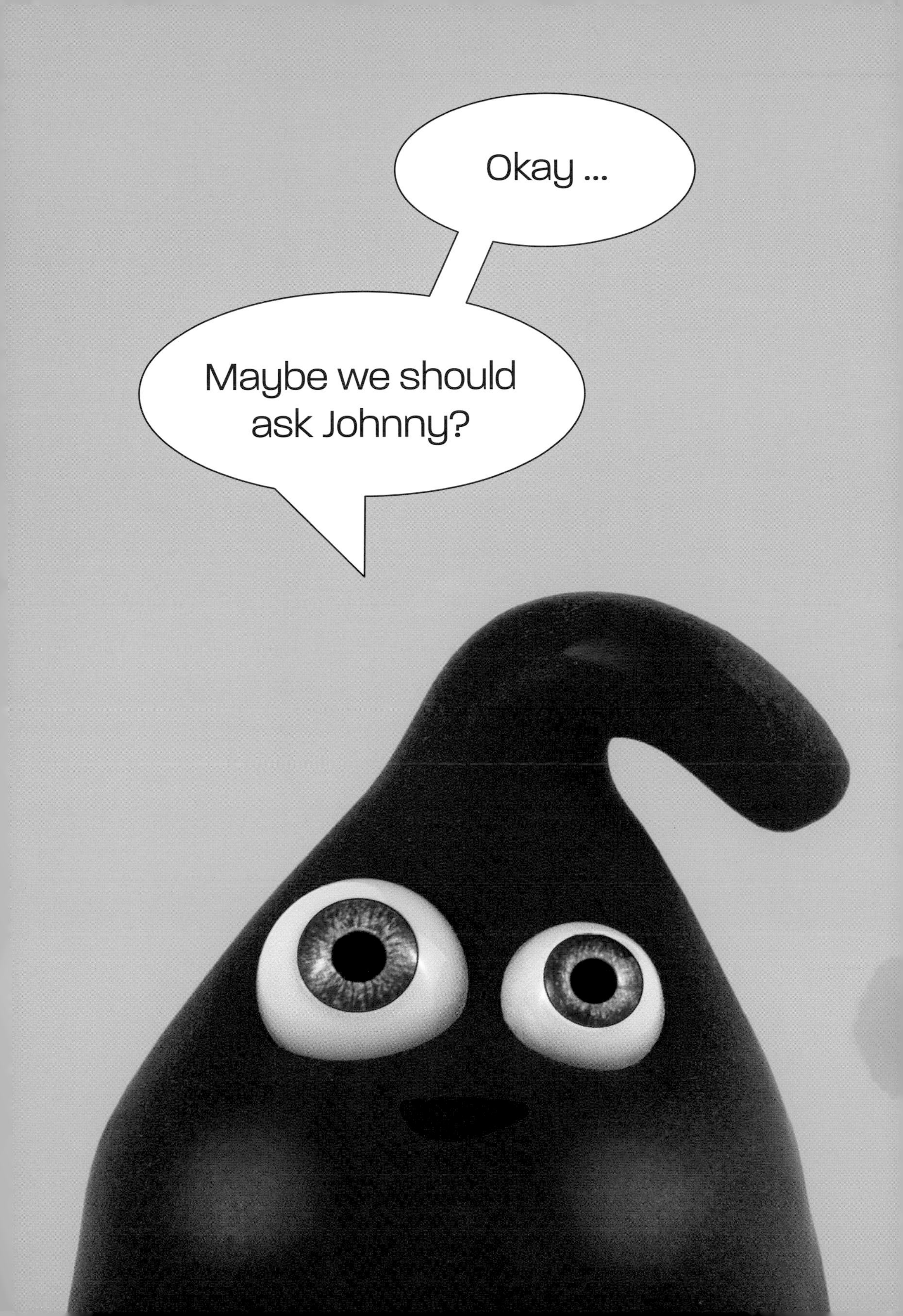
Okay ...
Maybe we should ask Johnny?

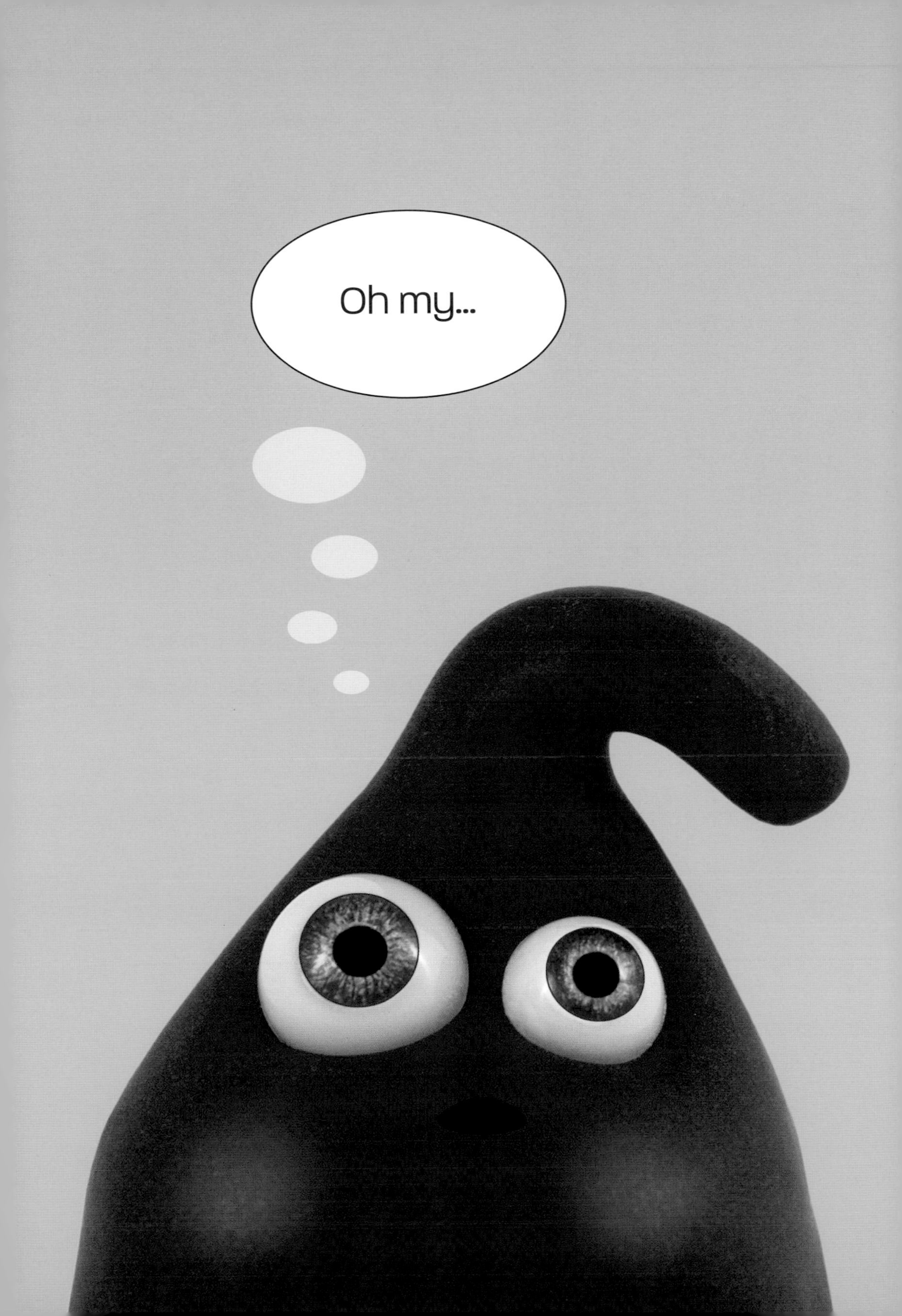
Oh my...

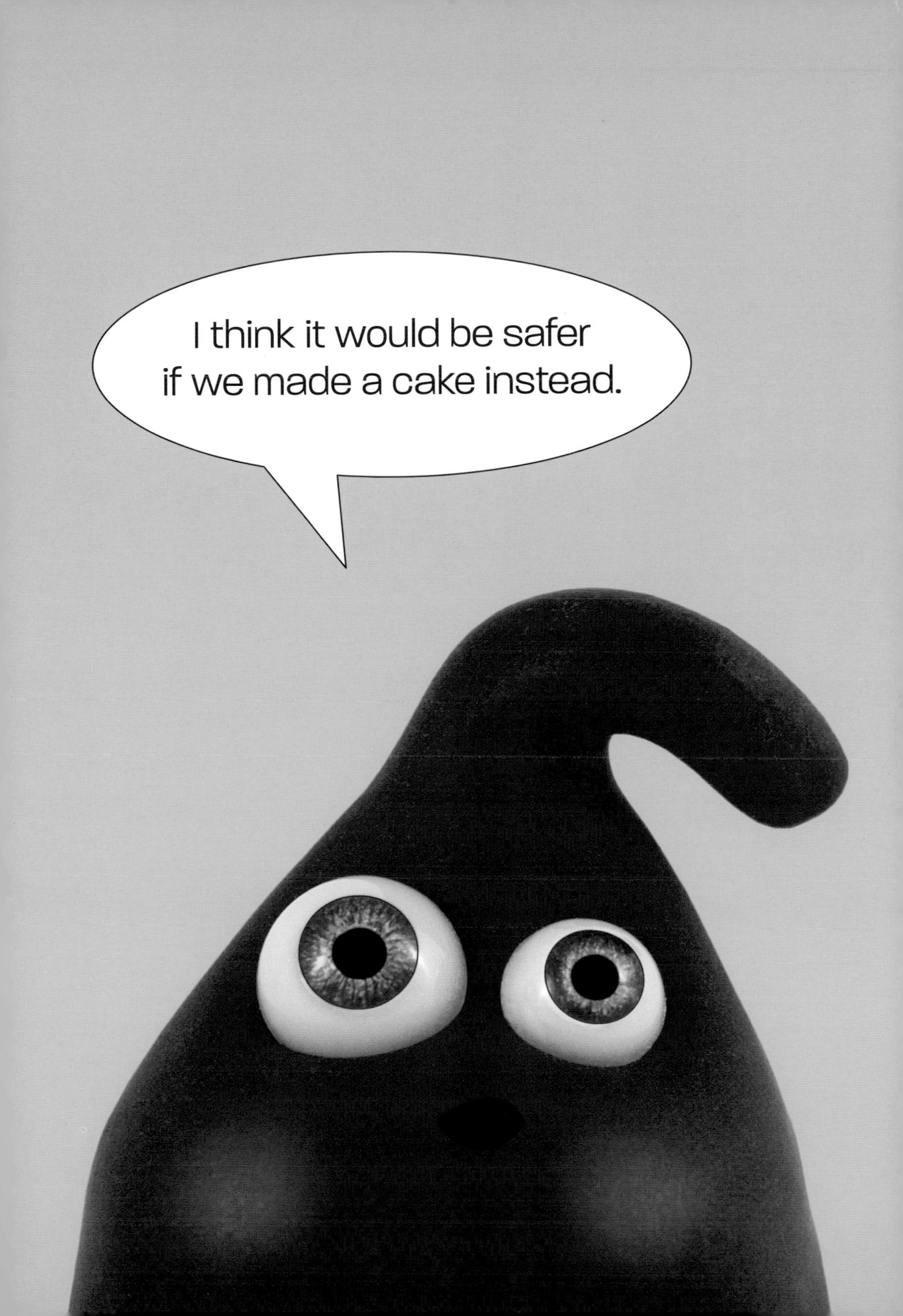
I think it would be safer if we made a cake instead.